Mary L. B. Foster

One Line of the Burritt Family

Mary L. B. Foster

One Line of the Burritt Family

ISBN/EAN: 9783337313449

Printed in Europe, USA, Canada, Australia, Japan

Cover: Foto ©Andreas Hilbeck / pixelio.de

More available books at **www.hansebooks.com**

ONE LINE OF

THE

BURRITT FAMILY.

"Let all unite, for the benefit of all, in placing upon record and preserving a recollection of our remote beginnings. Posterity will thank us for the labor, and the older the record grows the more value will they place upon it."—Welch.

ONE LINE

OF THE

BURRITT FAMILY.

---

1. William from Wales.
2. John, b. ———.
3. Joseph, b., 12 Mar. 1685,
4. Samuel, b., 1729.
5. Joseph, 9 Aug., 1758.
6. Joseph, b. 21 Aug., 1795.
7. Charles D. Burritt, b. 29 May, 1823.
8. Mary Lord Burritt Foster, b., 1848.
9. Jesse W. Foster, b. 1880.

Compiled By Mary L. Foster.

WEST HILL PRESS,
ITHACA, NEW YORK.
1898.

JOSEPH BURRITT.

ONE LINE

OF THE

BURRITT FAMILY.

---

1. William from Wales.
2. John, b. ———·
3. Joseph, b., 12 Mar. 1685,
4. Samuel, b., 1729.
5. Joseph, 9 Aug., 1758.
6. Joseph, b. 21 Aug., 1795.
7. Charles D. Burritt, b. 29 May, 1823.
8. Mary Lord Burritt Foster, b., 1848.
9. Jesse W. Foster, b. 1880.

Compiled By Mary L. Foster.

WEST HILL PRESS,
ITHACA, NEW YORK.
1898.

"Let all unite, for the benefit of all, in placing upon record and preserving a recollection of our remote beginnings. Posterity will thank us for the labor, and the older the record grows the more value will they place upon it."—Welch.

ONE LINE OF

THE

BURRITT FAMILY.

THE
BURRITT FAMILY.

He who has traveled in Wales delights to have memory linger, not only on the beautiful hills and charming vales, but among those old ruins which make fair Wales so famous. Those remains of Roman encampments, hill fortresses, castles, castellated mansions and specimens of antique military architecture. And still memory loves to linger on the charming valley of Glamorganshire, so famed for its picturesqueness, and owing to its great fertility, often called "the garden of Wales." It is a section of country having to do with most ancient history way back in the days of the Romans.

Glamorganshire was inhabited by the Silures, which in succeeding ages was an independent principality, but was in 1033 overrun and divided by some of William's Norman nobles. About the time of the Conquest, and not long after the period of the revocation of the edict of Nantes, there was a great importation of new names into England and Wales. It was at this time that Barrat was first found in their nomenclature, a name that since became modified, some families retaining the old form, but others making changes, until the Barrat of centuries ago has become the Burritt of today. The surname Barrat was one of characteristic, and it meant the "cunning." Not in the sense of craftiness, but having reference to their skill in doing things. In looking over the history of the old time Barrats, so

many have been found to be watch-
makers, jewelers and skilled workers,
that it would seem that they still retain
the ancient cunning that gave them their
surname, way back in the early days following the Conquest.

As early as 1550, a scholar at Cam-
bridge spelled his name both Barret and
Baret, being known later as a distinguished traveller, and author of a tripple dic-
tionary in English, Latin and French,
which he entitled an "Alvearie," as
the materials were collected of his
pupils in their daily exercise, like so
many diligent bees, gathering honey to
their hive. This book appeared in 1573.
The author died in 1580.

In 1801, in Nottinghamshire, we find
one Zachariah spelling his surname Bar-
ratt;—still the cunning, as he that year

invented a wonderful machine for grinding grain, either by water, wind, horse, hand or otherwise. Seventeen years after (1818), this same Zachariah had changed his name to Barrat.

In 1776, we find still another spelling, Geo. Barret. He was one of the Vice Presidents of the Society of Artists in Great Britain, as incorporated entitled as follows:—"The Society of Artists of Great Britain." Arms; upon a field azure a brush, a chisel, and a pair of compasses composed fretty, or: over them in chief a regal crown, proper: supporters, on the Dexter side, Britannia; on the sinister, Concord; crest on a wreath, an oak branch and a palm branch in saltire, in the center of which a chaplet of laurel. That same George received a prize of 50 guineas for his landscape painting.

In another line we find Thomas Barret a principal officer to his highness Omduc ul Omrah, nabob of Arcot and its dependencies, who died at his palace of Chepauk.

We find also a James in Saffron Walden, who spelled his name Barrett, an iron monger who had received patents: and so it seems that whether Barat, Barrett, Barrat, Barret, Baret, Burritt or Burrett, there has ran through all branches the cunning handiwork which originally gave to the family their name.

This change in the orthography of a name was nothing unusual. Today, frequently, we find different branches of the same family spelling their names differently; [Farley has had eleven different spellings] as instance in Ayoub we recognize the name Job, Abraham in Ibra-

him, Solomon in Souleimon. When
learned men in Germany wrote Rheabe-
am and Zitkias, and in France, Roboam
and Sedecios [Rehoboam and Zedekiah]
they both mean to designate the same two
individuals, viz., the son of Solomon and
the last king of Judah. The common an-
cestor of the Burritt family in America
was William Burritt of Glamorganshire,
Wales, who settled, with his wife Elizabeth, in Stratford, Connecticut where he
was one of the earliest settlers, and where
he died in the year 1651. John W.
Thompson, the historian of Stratford,
states that the inventory of his estate,
May 28th, 1651, amounted to £140. His
relict Elizabeth died in 1681, and the
history makes mention of three children
as follows :—

   i.   Stephen, Lieutenant, m, Jan 28, 1673-4, Sarah, daughter of Isaac Nichols : d. 1697-8 ; had eight children.

2. ii.   JOHN.

   iii.   Mary, m.—-Smith.

JOHN[2].

John, son of Wm. and Elizabeth Burritt, m. 1st, Deborah Barlow, May 1, 1684. He married, 2nd, Hannah Beach, widow of Zechariah Fairchild, May 5, 1708. He d. Feb. 1. 1726-7. He had—

3. JOSEPH. b. March 12, 1685

TRIBE OF JOSEPH BURRITT (3) AND MARY WAKELEY.

Joseph, son of John (2) and Deborah (Barlow) Burritt, m. Nov. 25, 1708, Mary Wakeley. Her grandfather, Henry Wakeley, was among Stratford's first settlers. He had six children, James, Deliverance, Jacob, Abigail, who married John Beardsley, Patience, who married Timothy Titterton, Mary and Mercy. Either Mary or Mercy married Samuel Gregory.

Deliverance, Dec., 3, 1678, m. Hannah Nash, and their sixth child, Mary, b. 3 March, 1688-9, became the wife of Joseph, 3. Hannah Nash was the daughter of Edward Nash of Stratford. She was born Jan. 18, 1651.

The children of Joseph Burritt and Mary Wakeley are as follows :—

   i. John, b. Sept. 7, 1709.

   ii. Hannah b. Dec. 3, 1711 ; m. Israel Beach.

   iii. Joseph, b. June 23, 1719.

   iv. Deborah, b. Sept. 21, 1714 ; d. Jan. 4, 1716-17.

   v. Deborah, b. Feb. 3, 1716-17.

   vi. Mary, b. Sept. 22, 1721.

   vii. Nathan, bapt. May 13, 1721.

   viii. William ⎫
                ⎬ b. Dec. 28, 1726.
   ix. Ebenezer ⎭

4. x. SAMUEL, bapt. Nov., 1729.

TRIBE OF SAMUEL BURRITT [4]
AND MERCY BURTON.

Samuel, son of Joseph and Mary (Wakeley) Burritt, m. Mercy Burton, in 1757.

Solomon Burton married Mercy, dau. of Jeremiah Judson, Aug. 1, 1687. She was born in 1665, and her 3d child was Judson, who married Eunice Lewis, 9 January, 1721. Among the 11 children mentioned was Mercy, who married Samuel Burritt. Eunice Lewis, wife of Judson Burton, was the 11th child of Benjamin Lewis, the first of the name in Stratford. He married there Hannah, daugh-

ter of Sergeant John Curtiss, and settled
at Wallingford, and returned to Stratford
about 1675. She died in 1728, aged 74.

The children of Samuel Burritt and
Mercy Burton were as follows :—

  5. i. JOSEPH, b. Aug. 9, 1758.

     ii. Eunice, b. Dec. 21, 1760.

    iii. Nathan, b. June 6, 1763; m.
          Sarah—, 1791.

    iv. Ann Mary, b. July, 1770.

TRIBE OF JOSEPH BURRITT [5]
AND SALLY UFFORD.

Joseph (5), was born at Stratford, Ct., and served as a private in the War of the Revolution. His full term of service according to the pension application entered by his widow, was 17 months and 15 days. A portion of this service was under Captain George Benjamin, in Col. Samuel Whiting's Brigade. He died Oct. 3, 1830. His widow made application for pension on Oct. 14, 1836, at which time she was 74 years of age and residing at Stratford.

Thomas Ufford came from England in 1632 with his wife Isabel and three child-

TRIBE OF JOSEPH BURRITT [6] AND ASENATH CURTISS.

Joseph (6), b. Aug. 21, 1795, served a long apprenticeship to a watch repairer and silversmith at East Haven, Ct., who was a master of his calling. Here was constructed the tower clock which still marks the flight of time at Yale College. Here was also built and repaired the mathematical, optical and nautical instruments for all that country round about. Mr. Burritt thus became a proficient workman. June 17, 1816, he was married to Asenath Curtiss of East Haven, and in October of the same year, they left Stratford, Ct., in a one horse wagon, for Ithaca, N. Y., where they arrived after a journey of ten days. Here he entered

CHILDREN OF JOSEPH BUR-RITT [5] AND SARAH UFFORD.

    i. Samuel, b. Dec. 18, 1778.

    ii. Ann Mercy, b. July 18, 1781; m. William Peet.

    iii. Sally, b. March 4, 1783: m. Isaac Brooks, Aug 17, 1800.

    iv. David, b. Jan. 7, 1785; m. Anna Wells, Oct.28, 1807.

    v. James, b. Jan. 11, 1787; m. Betsey—, April 8, 1812.

    vi. Isaac, b. June 1, 1789; had three wives; m. 1st.July 29, 1811.

    vii. Joseph, b. Feb. 9, 1791.

    viii. Julia, b. Nov. 16, 1792; died young.

6. ix. JOSEPH, b. Aug. 21, 1795.

Martha Nettleton of Branford, and had eight children. Samuel, b. 21 January, 1670, afterwards Lieutenant, married Elizabeth Curtiss, Dec. 4, 1694. He died in 1746, aged 77 years. Lieut. Samuel and Elizabeth Curtiss his wife had 13 children. The youngest, Ebenezer, b. 1719, m. Nov. 17, 1743, Jane Moss, dau. of John and Jane Moss. They had Mehitabel, Samuel and Sarah; and Sarah, b. Feb. 19, 1760, m. Joseph Burritt 1778.

dren in the ship Lion, and landed at
Boston, where he was made a freeman
that same year. He was in Milford as
early as January, 1645, where he and his
wife Isabel joined the church in that
place. He died in Stratford in 1660,
leaving an estate of £.89, 12s, 7p. Had
three children; Thomas, John and a
daughter, who married Roger Terrell.
the children being born in England.
Thomas owned land in Wethersfield in
1641, and he married there Frarces,
daughter of the first Thomas Kilborne,
who outlived him, and her estate was
divided in January, 1684. His estate
amounted to £183¼.

John, son of Thomas and Isabella Ufford, married 1st, Hannah Hawley, sister
of Joseph Hawley, who came from Par-
wick, Derbyshire, England, and landed
near Boston, Mass., in 1629; and 2nd

into partnership with Wm. P. Burdick
with whom he was associated in business
for nearly a quarter of a century. He was
a member of the Aurora street M. E.
church for over fifty years, and most of
that time an official: for long the oldest
living member of No. 2 fire company; a
Free Mason; an overseer of the poor; a
trustee of the village and academy, and
director of the Tompkins county National
Bank; for some thirty years treasurer of
the Ithaca Mechanics' Society. He was
twice married, his 2nd wife being Lucinda, widow of Mr. Vandyke of Covert, N.
Y. The organ of the jeweler's trade, the
Jeweler's Record, in 1883, claimed for
Mr. Burritt that he was the oldest living
jeweler in the United States. He died
March 9, 1889. His 2nd wife died Feb.
2, 1867.

CHILDREN OF JOSEPH BURRITT
[6]

By 1st wife Asenath Curtiss :—

    i. Joseph Curtiss, b. Jan. 26, 1817.

    ii. Mary Ann, b. Dec. 15, 1819; d. March 20, 1821.

    iii. Susan Jane, b. Sept. 20, 1821.

7.   iv. CHARLES David, b. May 29, '23.

    v. William Henry, b. Nov. 27, 1824; d. March 12, 1825.

    vi. Mary Ann, b. June 29, 1826.

    vii. Benjamin, b. Aug. 27, 1828; d. Sept. 9, 1828.

viii. Caroline Amanda, b. Sept. 12,
1829.

ix. Sarah Cornelia, b. June 19, 1833.

x. Frances Maria, b. May 7, 1838.

By wife Lucinda :—

ix. Amelia Eliza, b. Jan. 24, 1848.

JOSEPH CURTISS BURRITT [7].

Joseph (7) entered into partnership with his father in the jewelry business May 1, 1838. He was one of the five trustees appointed to incorporate the second Methodist church of Ithaca in 1851, and remained a useful member to the day of his death. He was twice married; 1st to Hetty Maria Lord, daughter of Harley Lord, Jan. 30, 1839; 2nd, Julia Atwater, daughter of Leonard Atwater of Ithaca, Jan. 7, 1875. He died May 22, 1889.

DESCENDANTS OF JOSEPH [7].

By first wife :—

i. Ellen Maria. b. Jan, 1, 1841, m. William Henry Willson, July 11, 1860, and had—

    1. Fred William, b. Nov. 20, 1862.

    2. Herbert George, b. May 16, 1865; m. Oct. 2, 1889, Donna Louise, daughter of Wm. Freer of Ithaca.

    3. Carrie Bell, b. Nov. 21, 1870, d. Oct. 24, 1872.

ii. Edwin Joseph (8), b. Sept. 17, 1843, by trade a jeweller, m. Sep. 29, 1864, Louisa Minerva, daughter of John D. Weed. They had—

    1. Edwin Charles (9). b. April 5, 1866, a jeweler by trade, m. April 22, 1896, Lilla dau. of Samuel Kennen. They had—

        a. Frances Louise, b. Sept. 5, 1897.

iii. Hetty Eliza, b. May 14, 1847; m. 1st, Jan. 1, 1864, Ogden Hoffman Hall. He was born April 10, 1845, and died Jan. 10, 1871. She m. 2nd, Henry Townley, Oct. 30, 1873. She died Jan. 8, 1888. Children by first husband:

    1. Lizzie Sinclair Hall b. Jan. 28, 1865; d. May 28, 1868.

ELLEN BURRITT WILLSON.

2. William Burritt Hall, b. Feb.
19, 1866.   He was educated
in Boston as a musician, af-
terward completing his stud-
ies in Paris ; m. Feb. 26, '91,
Alice West Fielder, of Dansville, N. Y , b. July ? 1, 1866.
They had :—

    a. Edward Fielder, b. June
       18 1892.

    b. Harold Glenn, b. May
       16, 1894.

By second husband :—

3. Hettie Bell Townley, b. Sept.
3, 1874.

iv. Caroline Augusta, b. June 30, 1851,
m. Jan. 28, 1873, Edgar Avery
Atwater, of Ithaca.   They later
moved to Manchester, Iowa. They
had :—

1. Horace Burritt, b. Feb. 17, 1874.

2. Laura Ellen b. 2 March, 1876, m. June 9, 1897, Jesse Floyd Jackson, of Manchester, Iowa.

3. Florence Bell, b. Apr. 27, 1879.

Joseph C. Burritt (7) had, by second wife, Julia Atwater:—

v. Joseph Atwater (8), b. June 6, 1876, by trade a jeweler.

SUSAN BURRITT GAUNTLETT.

DESCENDANTS OF SUSAN JANE BURRITT (7) AND JOHN P. GAUNTLETT.

Susan Jane, daughter of Joseph Burritt (6) and Asenath Curtiss, m. March 7, 1839, John P. Gauntlett, who came from Portsmouth, England. She d. March 30, 1853. They had :—

  i Jane Asenath, b May 12, 1840; d. Nov. 13, 1858.

  ii. John Charles b. July 22, 1842, m. Oct. 16, 1879. Mary Celestia, daughter of Joseph McGraw of Ithaca, b. July 24, 1848. They had :—

1. Anna Jane, b. Oct. 20, 1880.

2. John McGraw, b. Oct. 22, 1882.

3. Minna Celestia, b. Nov. 23, 1884.

iii. Mary Olivia, b. Sept. 1, 1845; m. Arthur Benjamin Brooks, of Ithaca, a descendant of Sally Burritt (6) and Isaac Brooks of Stratford, Ct. They were married Sept. 22, 1870, and had :—

    a. Alfred Charles, b. July 28, 1871.

    b. John Gauntlett, b. Aug. 26, 1874.

Feb. 14, 1854, John P. Gauntlett m, 2nd Mary Jane, daughter of George Burritt of Stratford, Ct. He was a son of David Burritt (6). John Gauntlett d. May 8. 1879. They had :—

JOHN C. GAUNTLETT.

L.

MARY BURRITT GAUNTLETT

1. Katherine, b. Feb. 28, 1865,
   who m. Ira Place, Jan. 10,
   1893, and had :—
   a. Katherine, b. Oct. 3,
      1893.
   b. Herman Gauntlett, b.
      Nov. 16, 1894.
   c. Willard Fiske, b. June
      5, 1896.

CHARLES D. BURRITT [7].

Charles David Burritt (7), b. May 29, 1823, united with the First Methodist Church of Ithaca, N. Y., under the labors of Rev. Schuyler Hoes, in January, 1841. Soon after he went to college at Middletown, Ct., and in 1843 he graduated as Bachelor of Science. During the following winter he returned to Middletown as tutor, and remained until August, 1845, and having completed his course of study in the languages, was admitted to the degree of Bachelor of Arts. He ranked high in Mathematics. He had calls to teach in five different institutions of learning, but

REV. CHARLES D. BURRITT.

felt that he was called to preach the gospel, and accordingly, in 1844, he joined the Oneida Conference. His first pastorate was at McGrawville, and succeeding ones at Skaneateles, Norwich, Ithaca, Cazenovia, and again at Ithaca, remaining the full term two years, at each, except at Norwich, and Ithaca the second time. He was eminently a successful preacher, and wherever he labored, revivals were witnessed. In the spring of 1850, he, with others, resolved that the time had arrived for the formation of a new society in Ithaca. A Sunday school was accordingly started, in the part of town where the church was to be located, followed by a class, of which the leader was Mr. George Young. Finally, on the evening of the third of February, 1851, the Second Methodist Church of Ithaca

was incorporated   In 1855, on account
of failing health, he was obliged to leave
the ministry, and in August of that year
he moved to Delaware, Ohio, to become
President of the Wesleyan Female Seminary. The following February he was
compelled to resign, and returned to Ithaca, where he died, at his father's, Mr.
Joseph Burritt's, on Wednesday, May 7,
1856, at a quarter past eleven in the
morning, aged 32 years, 11 months, 8
days. The funeral was Friday, at 2
o'clock. He was twice married; first,
August 27, 1844, to Jerusha Webster
Lord, daughter of Harley Lord, who d.
Feb 17, 1854, at Cazenovia. He m. second, Orpha Iantha Randall, daughter of
Joshua Randall of Camden, N. Y., Nov.
19, 1854.

Children by wife Jerusha W. Lord:

MARY LORD BURRITT FOSTER.

i. Mary Eliza, b. at Middletown, Ct., May 31, 1845, d. Aug. 9, 1845.

ii. Charles Paddock, b. July, 1847, at Havana, N. Y., d. Aug., 1847.

iii. Mary Lord (8), b. Sept. 7, 1848, at Skaneateles, N. Y. On the death of her father, she went to live with her grandparents, Mr. and Mrs. Lord, and her aunt Mrs. Herrick, with whom she remained most of the time until her marriage, living successively in Dansville N. Y., Lyons Iowa, Maquoketa Iowa and Ithaca N Y. July 14, 1874, she m. George E. Foster of Milford, N. H., and had :—

  1. Jesse Webster Foster, b. 11 Feb., 1880.

iv. Emma Eliza, b. Oct., 1850, d Aug. 1851.

Charles D. Burritt had, by 2nd wife, Orpha I. Randall :—

v. Charles Randall (8), b. Oct. 8, 1855, at Delaware, Ohio. He be- came a jeweler, and m. Sept. 19, 1883, Emma Presher, of Ithaca, and is residing at Canestota, N. Y. They had :—

    1. Nina May, b. May 2, 1885, at Ithaca, N. Y.

    2. Edna, b. July 26, 1888, at Sayre. Pa

MARY ANN BURRITT. [7]

Mary Ann Burritt (7), b. June 29, 1826, m. 1st, May 1, 1851, Ellsworth S. VanHoesen, who d. Dec. 29, 1853. She m. 2nd, Charles W. Smith, March 17, 1859; he d. Dec. 10, 1887. She d. Dec. 12, 1892. No issue.

DESCENDANTS OF CAROLINE A. BURRITT [7].

Caroline Amanda Burritt (7), m. Horace Augustus Merriam, Sept. 20, 1853. He d. August. 3, 1879. She d. Jan. 4, 1893. They had :—

    i. Charles Burritt (8), b. June 4, 1854 d. Sep. 3, 1854.

    ii. Franklin Asbury (8), b. June 7, 1857, m. Feb. 6. 1891, Eva Belle, daughter of William H. Sickles, of Newark, N. J. Mr.

Merriam was an employee in the office of the Ithaca, N. Y. "Journal," and afterwards took an editorial position on the "Argus", Mount Vernon, N. Y. becoming, in 1897, one of the proprietors.

iii. Ella Bell (8). b. Dec. 8, 1859. m. Dec. 16, 1879. Theodorus Van-Wyck, of Mont Vernon. They had :—

    1. Harold Van Wyck. (9), b. July 14, 1882.

iv. Frederic Lincoln (8), b. July 9, 1865, m. 10 June, 1897, Lillian Eugenia, daughter of Lorin Clark of Mount Vernon, N. Y. Mr. Merriam is a clerk in the New York Central Depot.

Sarah Cornelia (7) m. Jan. 11, 1854, Charles F. Williams. She d. Oct. 4, 1868. They had :—

1. Cornelia F. (8), b Oct. 4, 1868, unmarried, and a teacher in the public schools of Ithaca, N. Y.

CHARLES R. BURRITT.

MARY ANN BURRITT. [7]

Mary Ann Burritt (7), b. June 29, 1826, m. 1st, May 1, 1851, Ellsworth S. VanHoesen, who d. Dec. 29, 1853. She m. 2nd, Charles W. Smith, March 17, 1859; he d. Dec. 10, 1887. She d. Dec. 12, 1892. No issue.

DESCENDANTS OF CAROLINE A. BURRITT [7].

Caroline Amanda Burritt (7). m. Horace Augustus Merriam. Sept. 20. 1853. He d. August. 3. 1879. She d. Jan. 4. 1893. They had :—

    i. Charles Burritt (8), b. June 4. 1854 d. Sep. 3. 1854.

    ii. Franklin Asbury (8). b. June 7, 1857. m. Feb. 6. 1891. Eva Belle, daughter of William H. Sickles, of Newark, N. J. Mr.

Merriam was an employee in the office of the Ithaca, N. Y. "Journal," and afterwards took an editorial position on the "Argus", Mount Vernon, N. Y. becoming, in 1897, one of the proprietors.

iii. Ella Bell (8), b. Dec. 8, 1859, m. Dec. 16, 1879, Theodorus Van-Wyck, of Mont Vernon. They had :—

    1. Harold Van Wyck, (9), b. July 14, 1882.

iv. Frederic Lincoln (8), b. July 9, 1865, m. 10 June, 1897, Lillian Eugenia, daughter of Lorin Clark of Mount Vernon, N. Y. Mr. Merriam is a clerk in the New York Central Depot.

SARAH CORNELIA BURRITT. [7]

Sarah Cornelia (7) m. Jan. 11, 1854, Charles F. Williams. She d. Oct. 4. 1868. They had :—

1. Cornelia F. (8), b Oct. 4, 1868, unmarried, and a teacher in the public schools of Ithaca, N. Y.

FRANCES BURRITT KENNEDY

FRANCES MARIA BURRITT [7].

Frances Maria (7) m. April 14, 1859,
Laurence P. Kennedy. She d.
April 2, 1894, aged 55. They
had :—

1. Alvah Burritt Kennedy (8), b. 17
March, 1864, a jeweller by
trade, m. May 30, 1895, Nellie
Grace, daughter of Prof. Works
of the Wesleyan Seminary at
Lima, N. Y. They reside in Ithaca, N. Y. They had ;—

a. David Works, b. Feb. 19,
1897, d. March 27, 1897.

DESCENDANTS OF AMELIA ELIZA BURRITT [7] AND GEORGE E. PRIEST.

Amelia Eliza (7) m. Oct. 22 1865, George E. Priest, who has for many years been connected with the Ithaca "Journal." He has shown unexceptional talent as its editor, and has conducted the political columns of his paper with ability and shrewdness. He has had the satisfaction of seeing his paper take high place in interior city journalism. They had :—

1. Louise V. (8), b. at Ithaca, Sept. 1, 1867, m. Edward E. Ingalls, of Ithaca, March 22, 1887.

GEO. E. PRIEST, EDITOR OF ITHACA JOURNAL.

AMELIA BURRITT PRIEST.

2. Jesse E. (8), b. at Ithaca. Jan 2,
    1870, m. April 8, 1890, Wm. T.
    Armstrong of Mount Vernon, N.
    Y., who for some years has been
    local editor of the Ithaca "Journal"
    and correspondent for the New
    York "Sun" and other metropolitan
    papers.
3. Maud Winifred (8), b. at Ithaca,
    Sept. 1, 1877.

A REFLECTION

In concluding the record of this single branch of the descendants of William, who came to this country from Glamorganshire, it is of interest to note the irreproachable standing of the family through the various generations. Their record has been one of industry. They have been religiously inclined, and often active in church work. The family do not forget that the immortal Elihu was of the same ancestral blood. Indeed, the same indomitable pluck that he displayed in gaining his education has manifested itself in many members of the several branches of the family in this country. Indeed, in our own branch it was well illustrated by the early struggles of that pioneer jeweller and watchmaker in Ithaca, Joseph Burritt:

and was further evidenced in the zealous
labors of his son, Rev. Chas. D., whose
zeal for the cause of religion no doubt
brought too soon the close of what would
have been a most brilliant career. In this
country the family numerically is on the
decrease. Over in Wales, where once
dwelt the pioneer William, the ancestral
fields, once fertile and green, are today
covered by many homes. Strange names
are borne by the people who tread the
soil that the pioneer William bade fare-
well to more than two hundred and fifty
years ago. Country hamlets have given
way to bustling villages. In the shire
town of Glamorganshire the great Cardiff
library is the pride of Wales. Not long
since the gifted librarian of this famous
institution, at the request of the writer,
made search there for the name of some

living descendant of the ancestral race. Books of present pedigree, dwellings of all leading places in that populous county of Glamorganshire were carefully examined, people were inquired of, but not a single person could be found bearing the name of Burritt, a name that in England still exists in modified form,—it now only lives as an American name of what has become purely an American family.

FAMILY OF ASENATH CURTIS.

Asenath Curtiss became the wife of Joseph Burritt 6, (see page 16).

Phineas Curtiss (1) is the first member of the Curtiss family whose name is recorded in the town records of East Haven Ct. It is recorded that he married Hannah Russell, May 28, 1759. Their children were :—

i. Benjamin (2).

ii. Abigail (2).

iii. Phineas (2), who m. Mary Chedsey,
July 4, 1787, and d. 1806. They
had :—

   1. Polly (3), b. June 12, 1788.
   2. Hannah (3), b. March 17
      1790.
   3. Russell 3, b. March 16, 1792.
   4. Loly 3, b. Feb. 11, 1794.
   5. Asenath, b. Feb. 28, 1796:
      she m. Joseph Burritt, June
      17, 1816, and moved to Ith-
      aca, N. Y. She was the
      mother of Rev. Chas. D.
      Burritt, who married Jeru-
      sha Lord, and had Mary
      Lord Burritt. She m. Geo.
      E. Foster, and had Jesse
      Webster Foster. Asenath
      d. Feb. 7, 1844, aged 47
      years, 11 months.

6. Benjamin 3. b. March 19, 1798.
7. Major 3, b. Dec. 20, 1800, who m. Ellen————, and moved to Ithaca.
8. John 3, b. April 26, 1802.
9. Susan 3, b. Feb. 11, 1804; she became Mrs. Mix, and moved to Ithaca.
10. Street 3, b. 1806, d. 1808.

PEDIGREE OF ELIHU BURRITT.

THE LEARNED BLACKSMITH.

1. William and wife Elizabeth had :—;
   Stephen in the line of Elihu.

   John in line of Ithaca Burritts.
   Mary, the progenitor of many
   Smiths.

2. Stephen m., 1673, Sarah, daughter
   of Isaac Nichols, son of Francis
   Nichols, who was son of Sergt.

   Francis Nichols from England.
   He was a near relative of Col-
   onel Richard Nicolle, the first
   English Governor of New York.
   who belonged to the famous
   Horse Guards of London.

Stephen was confirmed Ensign of the
Traine Band, 1672 ; made recorder of
Stratford, 1673 ; made Lieutenant, 1675 :
also Commissary of Army ; chosen Town
Treasurer, 1689 ; Chairman of Committee
on Wolf-killing ; Town Auditor, 1690.

Children of Stephen and wife Sarah ;—

3.   Elizabeth, b. July, 1675.

William, b. 29 May, 1677.

Peleg, b. 5. Oct., 1679, in direct
line of Rev. Blackleach Burritt

Josiah, b. 1681

Israel, b. 1687.

Charles, 1689. In line of Elihu.

Ephriam, b. 1693 :

Charles (3) had—

Daniel,

Charles,

Elihu.

4.   Elihu (4) had Elihu,

Elihu (5) had Elijah, Elizabeth, Emily,
George and ELIHU, the learned Black-
smith.

PEN-ADDENDA.

THE BURRITT NAME.

In a previous chapter we have spoken
at length concerning the probable con-
nection of the Barrett and Burritt name.
A subsequent investigation proves con-
clusively that the proposition that the
name was of French origin is correct.
We have shown how the French names
were introduced into Wales at the time
of the revocation of the edict of Nantes.
Barrett is recorded as one of these
names. In the era of French surname
giving, there was unusual excitement
in the religious world. At the close of
the tenth century and the commence-
ment of the eleventh, the number of
persons bore a great disproportion to the
number of personal names, and it was
found necessary to add in all public
acts a distinct appellation for the sake

of identifying individuals. Such names
figure in great numbers in the records
of all kingdoms of christendom up to
the fourteenth century. By degrees
this means of remedying the confusion
became insufficient. Those sobriquets
which described physical and moral
qualities, habits, professions, and the
place of birth were imposed on many,
who bore the same name by baptism,
and it was about that time that hereditary surnames became indispensable.
It is said to be an unquestionable fact,
that the higher order of purpled pre-
lates, commonly called cardinates, had
its rise in the 11th century, yet it did
not acquire its stable and undisputed
authority of a legal council before the
following age and the pontificiate of
Alexander III. The cap and bonnet became a symbol of religious devoteeism
early in the eleventh century. In 1245,
Innocent IV. granted the Cardinals the
privilege of wearing the red cap as an
emblem of their readiness to shed their

blood for the Catholic faith. But the red cap was not permitted to be worn by any except the cardinalate.—The secular clergy were distinguished by black leathern caps, the regulars by knit and worsted ones. A very early Frenchman, Patroillet, was the inventor of the square hat so long worn by students of the French universities, it was to denote that they had acquired full liberty, and were no longer subject to the rod of their superiors, in imitation of the ancient Romans, who gave a "pileus" to their slaves in the ceremony of making them free, vocare servos ad pileum. It will be seen that of necessity cap making must have been a most important industry in the very era of surname making. Camden informs us that after local names the most in number have derived from occupations or professions. There was no profession, no employment that did not give its designation to one or to many families. Lower says the practice of borrowing names from various occupations of life is of high antiquity. "Thus the Romans had among them many persons, and those too of highest rank that bore names answering to "potters, painters, etc." These names became, as we have said, hereditary in the eleventh or twelfth centuries. At this time the manufacture of caps became a leading occupation. The work on the Cardinals' caps, the caps of clergy of lesser degrees, for physicians and students required the skilled workmen; it was a distinctive trade. Those who made them in France were called Barrette. The Barrette was pictured on the sign, and the cap makers were people much honored by the people. To be the capmaker for the Cardinals was something highly desirable. A picture of a barrette (cap) on the sign board, soon gave the name Barrette to him who made the caps. Had our William of Stratford been the capmaker during the 11th century, his surname would have become Barrette, or the skilled capmaker. After the names had become

hereditary in France, these capmakers
(Barrette) scattered into other countries,
our ancestors went to Wales, as is told
elsewhere in this volume, others went to
England and Germany, where their
names took various spellings still closely
resembling the word Barrette, the orig-
inal French. Mordaque in his famous
book on nomenclature says that the
etymology of hereditary names in England and Germany is generally the
same as in France and Italy. The cap
(Barrette) was still a leading business
sign during the twelfth, thirteenth and
fourteenth century, frequent mention of
it can be found in England, but it no
longer gave the name Barrette to those
who did business beneath it. The cap
was appropriated by people of other
surnames, as indicative of their business,
but the name Barrette still lived with
numerous spellings. The family of
Barrette, Barret, or kindred spellings
still continued to be noted for their
skill as cunning artificers and instead of

being makers of caps, weavers of hoods
as they were in the eleventh and twelfth
century, they now were inventors, they
were famous for their knowledge of
mechanism, just as the Ithaca families
are to-day—who are jewelers. Just
when our branch of the Barrette or Bar-
ratt family changed their family name to
Burritt is not exactly known, but it was
not done without a reason. The lineal
name has been always an honorable one,
a synonym of honesty and integrity.
It is very doubtful if the name Burritt
would have been in existence to-day if
it had not been for the arising of a class
of knaves that were given a sobriquet
that closely resembled the ancient name
of Barrette.   In the sixteenth and
seventeenth century the term barratry
became a by-word and synonym of
knavery throughout the world, they
who practiced barratry were often
for short called barrets.   In England barratry was the offence of
stirring up frequent suits and quarrels

among his majesty's subjects; in Italy
it was applied to the traffic of ecclesias-
tical beneficiaries and later it was applied to all corrupt buying and selling of
justice: in Scotland it signified the corrupt purchasing of beneficies or offices
of corruption from the see of Rome —it
was an act to prevent the free elections
of the monks in the monasteries.   In
France, any fraud practiced by the mas-
ters of vessels was accounted barratry
and severely panished.   It was a term
in England, and every commercial state
in Europe that had the meaning of
piracy, and was recognized by an act of
Congress of the United States as late as
1804.   It is nothing strange that the
term barratry and they who were called
barrett because they practiced it should
have been distasteful to the descendants
of the Barrette of France who felt a
pride in all that pertained to a long
established and honorable name, and
some families, our own included, desir-

ing to have in their name no semblance
of dishonor began calling themselves
Burritt, which was the name borne by
William who came to Stratford from
Glamorganshire at a time when barratry
was a term hated by all good citizens.